Copyright © 2005 by NordSüd Verlag AG, Gossau Zürich, Switzerland
First published in Switzerland under the title *Rapunzel*
English translation copyright © 2005 by North-South Books Inc., New York

First published in the United States, Great Britain, Canada, Australia, and New Zealand in 2005
by North-South Books, an imprint of NordSüd Verlag AG, Gossau Zürich, Switzerland.
Distributed in the United States by North-South Books Inc., New York.

Library of Congress Cataloging-in-Publication Data is available.
A CIP catalogue record for this book is available from The British Library.

ISBN 0-7358-2013-9 (trade edition)
1 3 5 7 9 HC 10 8 6 4 2
ISBN 0-7358-2014-7 (library edition)
1 3 5 7 9 LE 10 8 6 4 2

Printed in Italy

RAPUNZEL

A Fairy Tale by Jacob and Wilhelm Grimm

Illustrated by Dorothée Duntze

Translated by Anthea Bell

North–South Books

New York ❧ London

$\mathbf{T}$HERE WERE ONCE a man and his wife who had longed for a baby for many years, but in vain. Then, at last, it seemed that God was going to grant their wish.

The couple's house overlooked a wonderful garden full of the most beautiful flowers and herbs. The garden was surrounded by a high wall, and no one dared enter, because it belonged to a very powerful witch who was greatly feared.

One day the woman was standing at the window looking down into the garden, and she caught sight of a bed full of plants called rampion or rapunzel. They looked so fresh and green that she felt a great longing to eat some of them. Her craving grew stronger every day, and she pined so for the rampion that she wasted away to skin and bone, and became pale and miserable.

Alarmed, her husband asked, "What's the matter, dear wife?"

"Oh," she replied, "if I don't get some of those rampion plants, I am sure I'll die."

The man loved her, and he thought: rather than let my wife die I must fetch her some of that rampion, never mind what it costs.

So he climbed the wall of the witch's garden in the evening twilight, quickly picked a handful of rampion, and took it to his wife.

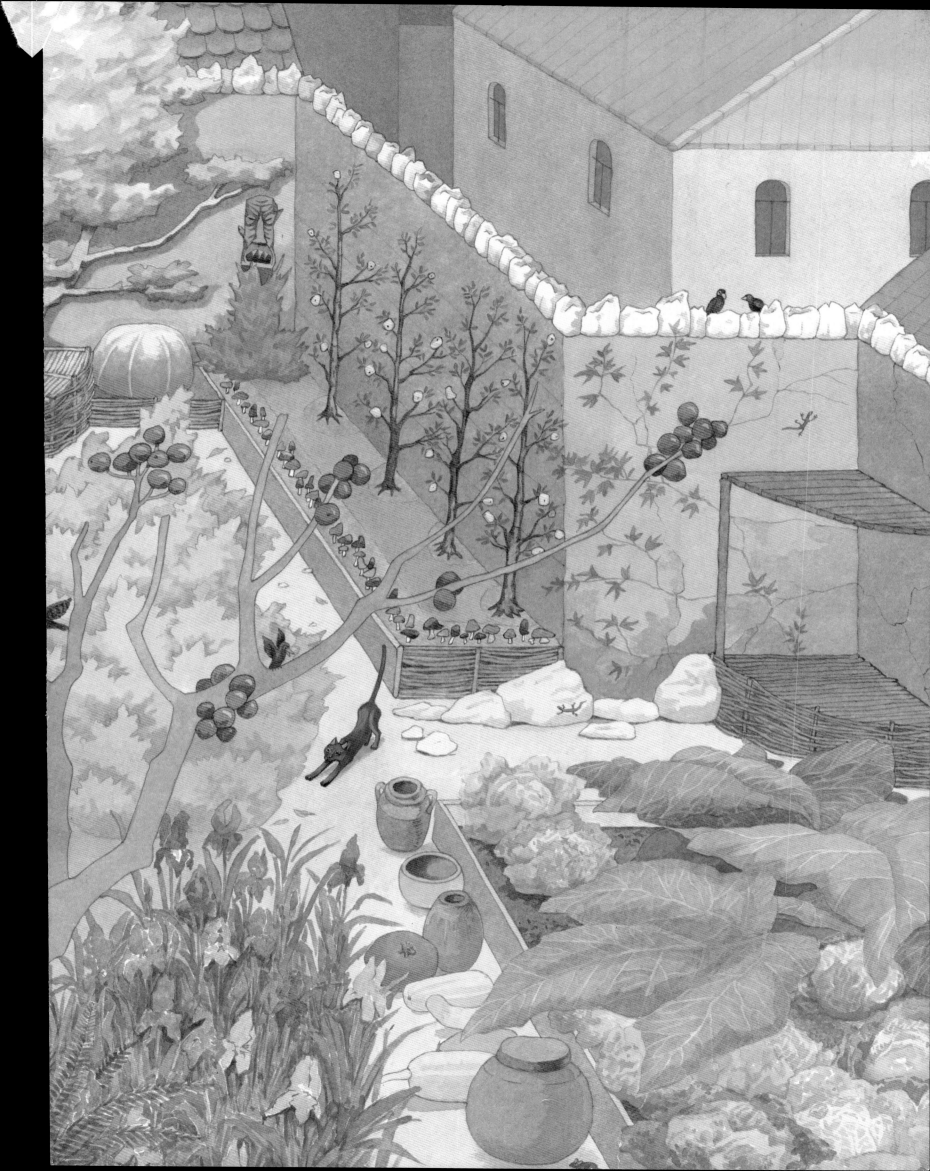

She immediately made it into a salad and ate it with a hearty appetite.

But the rampion tasted so good that she craved the herb three times more the next day. She begged her husband to climb into the garden again. So he set off in the evening twilight once more, but when he climbed down inside the wall he had a terrible fright, for there stood the witch!

"How dare you climb into my garden?" she shrieked angrily. "How dare you come here like a thief to steal my rampion? You'll be sorry for this."

"Oh, have mercy!" said the man. "I was forced to do it: my wife has seen your rampion plants from our window, and so longs for them that she will die if she doesn't get any."

Then the witch calmed down, and she said to him, "If what you say is true, then you may take as much rampion as you like, but I make one condition: when your wife has her baby you must give it to me. I'll look after it well and care for it like a mother."

In his fear, the man agreed, and as soon as his wife had borne her child the witch appeared, gave the baby the name of Rapunzel, and took the little girl away with her.

Rapunzel was the prettiest child in the world, but when she was twelve years old the witch shut her up in a tower that lay in the middle of a forest. It had no stairs or doors, only a little window very high up on the wall. If the witch wanted to come in, she stood at the bottom of the tower and called:

"Rapunzel, Rapunzel,
Let down your hair."

For Rapunzel had beautiful long hair, as fine as spun gold, and wore it in a braid. When she heard the witch's call, she wound her braid around a hook set into the window frame then let it drop to the ground, so that the witch could climb up it.

And the next day, as darkness began to fall, he went to the tower and called:

"*Rapunzel, Rapunzel,*
Let down your hair."

The hair immediately fell from the window, and the prince climbed up it.

At first Rapunzel was terrified when she saw him, for she had never seen a man before, but the prince spoke kindly to her, telling her how her singing had so moved his heart that it gave him no rest, and he had to see her for himself.

Then Rapunzel wasn't frightened any more, and when he asked if she would marry him, and she saw how young and handsome he was, she thought: he'll be kinder to me than my old godmother is. She put her hand in his and said, "I'll go with you happily. But it will be difficult for me to get out of this tower. Bring me a skein of silk every time you come to see me. I'll weave the silk into a ladder, and when it's finished I'll climb down it and you can take me away on your horse."

They agreed that he would visit her every evening because the old witch came only in the daytime. And the witch noticed nothing for quite a while, until one day Rapunzel said to her, "Tell me, Godmother, why are you so much heavier for me to pull up than the prince, who climbs up to me in just a moment?"

"Oh, you wicked child!" cried the witch. "What have you done? I thought I'd kept you shut away from the whole world, and now you've deceived me!"

In her anger, she grabbed hold of Rapunzel's beautiful hair, took a pair of scissors, and snip, snap, off came the beautiful braid. Then, she dragged poor Rapunzel into a bleak wilderness, abandoning her there to live in great misery and want.

On the evening of the day when she had banished Rapunzel to the wilderness, the witch fastened the braid she had cut off to the hook in the window frame, and when the prince came along and called:

"*Rapunzel, Rapunzel,*
Let down your hair,"

she let the braid fall. The prince climbed it—and at the top of the tower he found not his beloved Rapunzel but the witch, who looked at him with venomous malice.

"Aha," she said scornfully, "so you've come for your darling wife, but the pretty bird has flown the nest and won't sing any more, for the cat caught her and will scratch your eyes out too. You've lost Rapunzel, and you'll never see her again."

The prince was beside himself with grief, and in his despair he jumped out of the tower window. He escaped with his life, but the thorns into which he fell put his eyes out, blinding him. Then he wandered the forest, eating only roots and berries, weeping and wailing for the loss of his beloved Rapunzel.

So he wandered for several years, and at last he came to the wilderness where Rapunzel was living in poverty with the twin children she had borne him, a boy and a girl.

He heard a voice, and it sounded very familiar, so he followed it, and as he came close Rapunzel knew him at once, flung her arms around his neck and wept. Two of her tears fell on his eyes, and his eyesight was restored. Indeed, he could see even better than before.

So the prince took Rapunzel back to his kingdom,
where he was welcomed home with joy, and they lived
happily for many years to come.